the Dream Jar

by Lindan Lee Johnson

Illustrated by
Serena Curmi

Houghton Mifflin Company
BOSTON 2005

A special thanks to Eden Edwards,
the dreamiest editor a writer could
wish for her first book

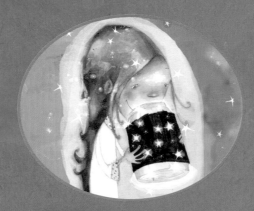

Text copyright © 2005 by Lindan Lee Johnson
Illustrations copyright © 2005 by Serena Curmi

www.houghtonmifflinbooks.com

The text of this book is set in Aunt Mildred and Jellybean, and with hand-lettering by the artist.
The illustrations were done in pencil and acrylic (on gray board), manipulated in Photoshop.

Library of Congress Cataloging-in-Publication Data

Johnson, Lindan Lee.
The dream jar / by Lindan Lee Johnson.
p. cm.
Summary: When a young girl has nightmares, her sister helps her by
sharing the secret of the dream jar.
ISBN 0-618-17698-5
[1. Nightmares—Fiction. 2. Dreams—Fiction. 3. Sisters—Fiction.] I. Title.
PZ7.J632524Dr 2004   [E]—dc22
2003017704
ISBN-13: 978-0618-17698-4
Printed in China
SCP 10 9 8 7 6 5 4 3 2 1

To my parents, Ed and Alice,
for always supporting my dreams, and my
daughters, Susannah and Mandalyn, for sharing
their own dreams with me
– L.L.J.

To my mum, my dad, and Matt
for always being
proud of me
– S.C.

My sister and I share a sky-blue room at the very tip top of the stairs.

My bed is on the left.

Her bed is on the right.

Our ceiling is covered with stars.

Every night Mom comes up to our room and we take turns reading a story.

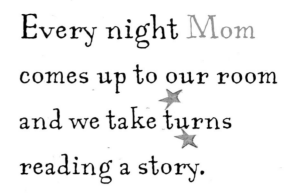

She tucks us in,

gives us a snuggle,

turns down the light,
and kisses us good night.

Then my
sister and I
go to sleep.

This is the way bedtime is SUPPOSED to be. But some nights it is NOT. Some nights I have BAD DREAMS and my sister has to save me.

My mom says I have a good imagination and this is just a stage I'm growing through.

I think I'd rather skip it.

My sister says I can save myself.

I think SHE'S the one with the imagination.

Because sometimes when NIGHT comes, my dreams

TURN REAL...

My bed is in the middle of the ocean!
SEA MONSTERS surround me!

YIKES!

"Wake up—you're only dreaming!"
My sister is shaking my shoulder.
I open my eyes and see my room—

NO ocean,

NO drowning teddy,

NOT a single sneaky
sea monster in sight!

"But it was SOOOO real!"

"Tell me about your dream," my sister says,
and listens to every scary word.

Then she lowers her voice.

"I think it's time to tell you

The Secret."

The Secret?

I LOVE secrets!

I bounce up and down on the bed.

"Tell me—tell me—tell me!"

"Mom told me this secret when I was your age. You can CHANGE the story of your dreams if you practice. Even if it starts out to be a BAD DREAM, you can make it into a good one . . . a Dreamy Dream."

Hmmm . . . what kind of secret is this?

My sister knows almost everything in the world — but THIS is very hard to believe.

"Let's start with your bad dream. It was about sea monsters—"

"VERY SCARY SEA MONSTERS!"

"Right. Now, can you imagine a sea monster that isn't scary?" asks my sister.

"That's IMPOSSIBLE. Sea monsters are always VERY SCARY.
It's their job."

"But sea monsters are not real," my sister says. "They are IMAGINARY.
So IMAGINE a sea monster that
isn't very scary."

"All right, I'll try.
Maybe if the sea monster
was teeny tiny it wouldn't
be very scary.

Or if the sea monster was really silly it wouldn't be SO scary," I say.

"You're right," says my sister. "Now close your eyes and see the really silly sea monsters in your mind. Make up a story about them. Turn your bad dream into a good one ... a Dreamy Dream."

This might just work.

My sister and I share a just-between-sisters yawn.

Now I can sleep, because my sister saved me.

My bed is in the
middle of the ocean,
surrounded by SILLY sea monsters!

One dives into the water
and rescues my bear.

Why, this silly sea monster's friendly.
He wants to play. I jump from my bed and
hop on, and the race to the waves begins!

Morning comes,
and the sun shines on me
in my bed on the left
of our sky-blue room
right at the top of the stairs.

It Worked!
My sister knows the secret
of Dreamy Dreams,
and she's always here
to save me.

Until—

without even a teensy WARNING—something TERRIBLY HORRIBLE happens.

My sister is invited to a SLEEPOVER.

"You can't go," I tell her. "We are a team! You need to be here to save me from BAD DREAMS. We can never ever *ever* be separated for the rest of our lives—*EVER!*"

"I have an idea," my sister says. "Let's make a list of things that make us laugh or feel good. Things we like to spend a long time thinking about."

playing leapfrog
with frogs

moonlight dancing
with fireflies

playing in the
park with lots of
puppies

taking over a toy factory

playing hide~and~seek
in a field of sunflowers

being invisible spies

thinking up 3 wishes
(and a fourth
one just in
case!)

discovering a new purple planet

having magical powers

"Tonight, you'll find the answer to your dreams," my sister tells me.

"Look for it when the lights go off."

She smiles her most MYSTERIOUS smile.

That was HOURS ago.
I check every clock in the house. *Finally* it's my bedtime!
I run up the stairs so fast my mother can't keep up.

"WHERE IS IT?
WHERE'S the answer
TO MY DREAMS?"

"Look on the nightstand," my mother says.

There on the nightstand next to the Laughing Moon lamp is a plain jar covered in dark blue paper.

I stare at the plain jar on the nightstand. I frown at the plain jar on the nightstand.

"Things are not always what they APPEAR to be," my mother says as she turns down the light.

Suddenly stars glow up on the
dark blue paper.
It takes my breath away.
"Your sister left you a note." It says:
Mom smiles. She must be remembering.

This is The Dream Jar
I made for you—
just like the one Mom
made for me!

When you are having a bad dream, The Dream Jar gives you
the power to wake yourself up. Reach inside and take out one
Dreamy Dream. Your mind will fill up with happy thoughts. Then
you can change the BAD DREAM into a good one.

I take off the lid and look inside. There are lots of tiny rolls of paper tied up with blue string, and little sparkling stars.

The Dream Jar is magic. I can feel it.

Mom reads me a story.
She tucks me in,
gives me a snuggle,
turns down the light,
and kisses me good night.

"But, Mom, I can't sleep by myself. The terribly horrible dreams will get me!"

"No, they won't," she says. "Your sister gave you The Dream Jar. You will know what to do."

Then she leaves me.

Alone.

I am NOT happy
about this.

I decide to stay awake all night.

The Dream Jar *glows* by the
light of the Laughing Moon.

My eyes feel very sleepy.

I'm in a dark, scary shopping mall. All the lights in the stores are blinking on and off!

I AM LOST!
Here is the escalator—
I want to go home.

YIKES!
THE ESCALATORS ARE ALIVE
AND THEY'RE
TRYING TO EAT ME!

HELP!

HELP!

HELP!

"Wake up—you're only dreaming," I hear my sister's
voice say. "Look inside *The Dream Jar!*"

I open one eye, but my sister isn't here.

Then I see The Dream Jar.

I take out one Dreamy Dream.

I untie the blue string and carefully unroll the little piece of paper. I read the tiny words my sister wrote just for me:

You have a
MAGIC WAND
— use it!

I smile and
close my eyes.

I am back in the shopping mall.

I point my MAGIC WAND
at the chomping escalators and they melt into
slippery, silvery slides that magically go
up and down and ALL AROUND!

On one of the slides, I see my sister. She laughs and waves at me.

"CONGRATULATIONS!
This is a fabulously FUN
Dreamy Dream!"

It IS a fabulously fun dreamy dream. I wave back, and we share a just-between-sisters smile. Then we soar off on double loop-de-loops on the slides shining with stars.

And when morning comes,
the sun shines on me
in my bed on the left
of our sky-blue room
right at the top
of the stairs.